Silent Forte

MJ Creed

Published by MJ Creed, 2024.

SILENT FORTE

First edition. December 26, 2024.

ISBN: 979-8230853824

Written by MJ Creed.

Table of Contents

Lost for Words

Ben

Dear Tessa, I hope this letter finds you well

The overhead light flicked off, causing my pen to drag on the holiday card as I attempted to write a simple note to Tessa. I glared into the darkness, knowing my hostile stare wouldn't intimidate the culprit who'd deliberately caused the ruin of one of my last few cards.

"Liora!" I grumbled to the spectral presence who found this prank so funny. Working at a haunted resort wasn't the fun that books and shows would make it out to be—especially when the spirits had a favorite tenant.

Tessa.

The onsite violinist was the reason I'd offered to fix the broken ice machine three years ago. Then I helped her with the radiator in her room that wouldn't work, and she was the reason I chose to remain here as the onsite mechanic. The woman's very presence in the evenings in the room next to mine was intoxicating. That captivating sensation wasn't the result of paranormal manipulations at a resort known to have a supernatural air of romance. This was all Tessa. And I was damned near about to go insane since she'd left on her winter trip over a week ago.

Despite how mad the otherworldly interference made me, I found no mercy when the Victorian-era electrical current hummed as the light flared back to life, revealing the jabbed mark where my pen had landed on the card. But worse than that eyesore, I had to see the words I'd chosen to write to her.

I tossed the elegant holiday card in the trash bin atop at least ten others. Only two more, so I had better do this right. I puffed air into my cheeks, blowing out before muttering under my breath. "I like you, Tessa." Those were the words anyone else in the world could speak. Words I should easily be able to express.

I picked up another card and gathered my pen in another attempt to write Tessa a note.

Dearest Tessa, you are such a wonderful

I didn't even need a spectral presence to stop me from finishing the sentence. That was the most ridiculous note so far. And *dearest*? That was sure to sound weird.

I sighed and tossed the pen onto the desk, cradling my forehead in my hands. I glanced over to the spot where I'd set my grandfather's antique violin on the floor. The beloved instrument didn't need to gather dust any longer. It wasn't like he could come to haunt me for giving it away. If anything, he would probably haunt me for not telling Tessa how I felt.

I sat up and crossed my arms over my chest. I never had success with women in all my life, and once here, the only woman I could imagine being with was Tessa, the violinist whose melody flowed through the cracks in the historic building. She was my personal haunting; I supposed. I certainly wouldn't write that in a note, though.

I picked up the pen again. *Just tell her I want her to have the violin, because it will just sit collecting dust otherwise. Tell her it has no personal value.*

Tell her the truth—

An inexplicable emptiness, worse than any physical ache, crept over me. One of those feelings that left a person wordless, though not because of any anxiety or surprise. And at times when I thought of Tessa, it always seemed to hit me the hardest. It was a new haunt to add to my recent collection of woes—one in the form of a decades-old holiday doll. A cloth angel, like so many that adorned mantles and shelves this time of year. Except, this one had been possessed by a specter—and it did watch people with those beady little painted eyes.

I looked over to the floor near the foot of the bed where it liked to appear. Sure enough, it sat slumped with its scuffed porcelain face in my direction. Christmas—the literal season of joy—was being attacked by its own mascot.

But not on my watch!

I yanked up the pen, glaring at the little monstrosity set on ruining any sanity I had left, not to mention how its presence seemed to heighten the tension in any room it was in. "You're on my list, doll. But so long as you're here, no other spirit will mess this card up." It was the only thing that the damned specter had in its favor for the next minute or two.

I kept the scuffed face in my periphery as I dragged the last card in front of me.

Tessa, Things haven't been the same here without you. I would love for you to accept this violin and use it for your upcoming performances.

I clicked the end of the pen and tossed it onto the desk, shifting my attention to the little doll, whose head was cocked sideways, watching me. More like taunting me with that creepy smile painted onto its face. As though it ridiculed what I'd written.

"That was your one free pass, doll," I grumbled, looking down to the card.

What was the worst response Tessa would express to the words I'd chosen? Politely refuse my gift? She would still sincerely smile and show appreciation, even if she refused.

I waited for the suffocating gloom to pass and puffed my cheeks with my next exhale. Now I just needed to wrap the violin and deliver it to her door before she returned this evening.

I opened my drawer and pulled out the sparkly white tissue paper and red gift bag, setting them out on my desk. Just as I was about to lean over for the violin, my phone vibrated from near the pen.

I swiped the screen, opening up a text from Mariah Prem. *Could you get out to the stables and scare off whoever snuck in?*

The workday hadn't even started, and the guests were already up to no good in an off-limits area.

I typed, *On it!*

She replied, *Thanks! I owe ya one for starting early.*

I gave the items on my desk an annoyed glance. Finishing wrapping the violin would be a job for my lunch break. For now, I had to start an early day of work at the historic lodge that seemed set on making sure I didn't finish this one simple task of getting a present to Tessa. I rapidly dressed and donned my heavy coat and toboggan and headed out to the old stables to see what kind of chaos Mariah had hinted at.

When I arrived, the familiar scent of old straw and decay hit me. I'd spent plenty of time in stables throughout my life and even here whenever horses were brought for events. But I'd never seen thick carrots snapped apart and laid out in a sacrificial way, as though they might magically reconnect. Someone had taken these perfectly good carrots and defiled them in some sort of ritual. What kind of guest would break into the stables just to do something so bizarre?

And why were there fresh coils of red rope and one of those crops used for riding horses resting on the stall gate? At least it was still in the plastic wrapper. Maybe they became disappointed to discover there weren't any horses onsite and tried to summon the ghost of one by performing some sort of vegetable sacrifice.

"Kids," I muttered under my breath, both annoyed and humored. What wouldn't I have done as an adolescent if stuck with family for the holidays at a resort rumored to be haunted, though?

I grabbed the unused equestrian items and stepped out of the stall. I still had time to get back and sneak a quick trip to wrap the violin for Tessa. Even get a cookie with buttercream frosting to add in.

The instant those ideas entered my mind, it was as if some unseen force had purposefully smashed them to bits. That damned angel doll had returned to torment me, and I wouldn't let it continue its spree of spreading misery.

I dropped the cords of rope and then ripped the plastic cover from the riding crop. "I warned you, doll." From the upper left corner of my eye, I saw the possessed doll slouched upon the loft. Those painted eyes seemed to glint with its delight at my discomfort.

I focused my sights on the possessed doll. With a forceful leap, I swatted the riding crop at it, knocking it downward from its perch on the loft and into the empty stall next to me. However, when I hurried over and peered over the thick wood fencing, the angel had already vanished. I clenched the crop's leather grip and scanned the shadowy stables, but there was no doll to be seen.

At least one good thing came of this trip out to the stables. In the right circumstances, this riding crop might turn out to be an excellent tool for catching that little spirit and sending it back to where it belongs.

Home, Transformed

Tessa

I'd become lost. Not in the sense of being unable to find my way, but lost in the beauty of the holidays. When I'd left Prem Proper over a week ago, it had been its usual romance destination, setting a scene for couples to fall in love. But my trip took me away from witnessing the Christmas transformation. That made this arrival all the more magical as I drank a peppermint mocha and passed surfaces adorned with crimson bows and velvet throes. I wandered, seemingly aimlessly, toward Christmas trees decked with shiny balls and garland, just to see if they were in every hall and banquet area. And, so far, they were.

It was time for me to set up in an empty banquet room and become lost in my music, immersing myself to be able to perform spectacularly in the festive setting. And, hopefully, see Ben—the Joseph Gordon-Levitt lookalike I ogled every chance our paths crossed.

No. I just needed to focus and become attuned to my surroundings and not think about the man who always caused my heart to skip a beat. I made my way into the nearest banquet room and placed my violin onto the round table, careful not to bump the crimson bow that was a place setting.

After removing my cherished instrument and my fragile bow from their case, I closed my eyes and gently placed the violin under my chin. My deep, centering breath captured the smell of cinnamon in the air. With a slow exhale, I drew the bow across the strings, welcoming the first notes into the festive banquet room. Now I could become lost in the music, letting my fingertips dance along the fingerboard as I played for none other than myself and the spirits that graced Prem Proper.

But somewhere in the middle of the piece, it felt as though the world shifted. As though the silence surrounding me became louder than the music, causing my hand to err, releasing a mournful shriek from the violin.

I opened my eyes, wondering what possibly could have caused the shift in the room. But it was an invisible shift, as though something unseen was missing. Maybe I just needed to focus on the tree and its glittery lights and bulbs.

I ran the bow along the strings again, sliding as smooth as silk, but again, something just wasn't right. I couldn't play Mozart, nor could I play Tchaikovsky or Bach. It was as if an invisible force was preventing me from playing. But I needed to get back into the state of mind to perform, especially in this new setting. With a deep breath, I let my fingers take over, and I couldn't have expected that such freedom would unleash the first notes to *Frosty the Snowman.*

I loved Christmas. It was my favorite time of year. The colors and smells. The love that seemed genuine, not like the short-term high people felt while at this resort as they fell head first for someone.

Real, deep love. Lasting love. The sort that reached into a person's soul.

And *Frosty* was *not* what I loved about Christmas. I puffed out a long breath of air, ready to close my eyes and try again, when I caught an odd glint from my periphery.

Perched atop the back of a black dining chair, a little dirt-scuffed angel doll watched me. Which I found quite odd.

Sure, anyone who'd been here long enough could believe that the haunting wasn't just weird occurrences like jammed doors and electrical interferences. But that doll definitely hadn't been there when I'd arrived—and it felt as though it was watching me. It bore the sort of painted on expression that met the definition of a smile, but the angles and curves of its mouth suggested no true joy at all.

But what was even stranger, the sensations I usually felt while in the lodge, like a warm and fuzzy blanket bundling me, had vanished. Not to say that the doll created a coldness, but the comfort I usually felt since my arrival here had passed. As though its very presence stole away the warmth and joy of the premises that had always grounded me to play at my very best.

I watched the possessed doll while lifting my bow to the strings, and I attempted Pachelbel. The instrument wailed, creating a sound that was at complete opposition with the slumped doll's painted on smile. One thing I knew for certain was that this little creature would be bad for business if its presence meant the drain of joy from the room.

Resolved to prevent any problems brought about by its arrival, I lowered my instrument and set it and my bow in the case, then went over and grabbed the doll. I used my sleeve to wipe the soot from its little face. Hopefully Mariah Prem, the owner of Prem Proper, would know what to do with it.

I packed up my violin and bow swiftly, eager to deliver this strange little doll somewhere safe before I had to perform later. My hurried steps had me rushing out the double doors, and my face collided with a firm shoulder.

As I lost balance, the man reached out with lightning speed, capturing me in one strong arm, and his other was quick to wrap me as well. It was breathtaking, both from the shock against such a rock-hard chest and the fact that those strong arms cradling me were those of Ben.

Even if I could speak, I wouldn't be able to. I wouldn't be able to do anything more than stare into his dark brown eyes that seemed so kind despite the fact that I'd just plowed into him. I couldn't even will my muscles to stand me upright. My attention went to the blackness above me where the flap of a riding crop curled downward.

"Tessa," he said, his concerned tone dragged me from my stupor. All too soon, he was lifting me upright again. "Tessa, I'm so sorry. I..."

Even after gathering my balance, I still stared at the crop he carried. I'd never considered him to be the sort of man who would be into the fetish lifestyle. Not that I knew anything about fetishes beyond books and television shows. But those characters never advertised their interests so openly.

He must have been surprised that I'd seen the crop, because he lowered it to his side. Maybe he didn't know what it was for. He might have just been taking it to the lost and found. I secretly hoped that was the case, simply because I didn't want to imagine him using it with a woman—let alone hear it in the room he occupied next to mine.

My violin.

The thought crushed the curiosity building within me. I stepped backward and signed a quick thank you to him and searched for my violin, which I hoped hadn't been damaged from the jostle.

Ben was the one to find it on the floor and pick it up. "Let me make sure it isn't damaged," he said, carrying it into the banquet hall to a large, round table.

I searched for the doll, but found nothing laying about on the polished floor. After a few long scans to places too far away for it to have landed, I followed him to the table near the tall Christmas tree.

My thoughts began to muddle as he walked with steady, controlled movements ahead of me. This man confidently held a fetish device. Luckily, this resort was an establishment for love, not kinks. Most everyone who worked here and came to vacation were the vanilla, love-desperate sorts of people. This month seemed different, though, with family holiday themes meant to bring out true joy. Either way, no one would know what it was that he carried.

Ben lowered the crop onto the table and then my violin case, which he opened and took the instrument out to examine it, checking every single part like an expert in the trade would. "It looks fine." He handed it to me. "Play it and I can see if it needs tuning."

I looked around to see if that angelic doll remained. I didn't feel the supernatural warmth of my surroundings that usually refreshed me, so the creature might still be nearby.

"Tessa." The way Ben said my name was so kind, yet in control. He extended the instrument to me, which I took from him. The slight, reassuring grin that reached his dark, almond-shaped eyes caused my stomach to flutter. It was a genuine smile that spoke dozens of words of kindness.

And I would feel horribly guilty if this caring gesture ended in me unable to play. He would probably blame himself for damaging my instrument or injuring me if my notes came out in a screech. I needed to let my hands choose.

I raised the violin into position and closed my eyes, and let my hand determine the tune. Notes poured out, filling the room with *All I Want for Christmas is You*. I didn't dare open my eyes. I just had to get through this and find that little creature whose presence still impacted me.

Only when the tune ended did I peek to see Ben watching me, just as he'd sometimes done before. This time, though, he was seated only feet away instead of near a wall at the far side of a room.

When our eyes met, I had no doubt a rosy glow overtook my cheeks. I lowered my violin and bow to my lap and ran a hand through my dark brown, shoulder length waves, suddenly self-conscious. Now, more than with the music, I missed the ethereal warmth of the lodge that usually shielded me from such fear of scrutiny.

"May I?" Ben asked, already reaching for my bow, but awaiting my response.

I'd thought I played the tune perfectly, but something must not have sounded right to him if he felt the need to inspect my bow.

I handed it to him, unable to take my gaze from his precise movements as he ran his fingertips along a recent repair I'd made.

He was still inspecting it when he said. "There's a crack."

The bow wasn't unusable yet, but it probably didn't have enough life in it to last beyond the season. I typed on my phone screen. *I'll order another next year.*

"I have one. If you would like." He sat upright in the seat and lay the bow on the table as he spoke, his attention toward the tree. "It's just something I kept around."

He'd always been kind to everyone, but this felt different—more personal. I liked it, but I couldn't take something special from him. Preferring friendly banter and a polite refusal, I typed, *No one keeps a bow around that isn't important to them.*

His head bobbed side to side, solemn perhaps. "It was my grandfather's." The pain of the loss still lingered in his eyes.

My attempt at lighthearted banter had inadvertently stirred up sorrow. It was a reminder that there was more than one reason I shouldn't bother with conversation. I gestured a somber apology.

"Thank you, Tessa," Ben said, "and the bow is yours if you want it." His eyes held a new intensity toward me as he stood, collecting his riding crop from the table. "There's something I need to take care of."

The way he held that crop made me wish it was me he felt the urge to take care of, even if it involved correcting my rude comment.

Crumbling

Tessa

Currently, no possessed doll stole away the comfort of the familiar spectral presence that resided within Prem Proper, so I decided to stop in at the dining room for an early performance. Only a handful of families were there with a few young children that played and babbled. Thoughts of my interaction with Ben were still jostling me as I set up to play my instrument.

I had to let the delight of the encounter sink in. Conversation wasn't something that happened—not with anyone. If I had something to express, people heard it in my performance. Or someone said whatever they had to say, then we all smiled, and I went about my day to perform or go to my room and play some more music to the spectral presence that loved to hear the melody.

I glanced to the far end of the festive room. In the past, Ben sometimes stood against the far wall for a few minutes to listen as I performed. He wasn't there now, though.

With a calming breath, I lowered the bow to the strings, releasing the uplifting power of Pachelbel, which danced in the air. Not even half a minute passed before the protective warmth surrounding me shrank away, leaving me unshielded and all too aware of the possible scrutiny.

A screech escaped my beloved strings.

The wail of a toddler in a red Christmas dress rang out.

My failed attempt to perform caused this disturbance in the otherwise peaceful and romantic lodge. I could mend that, though. I could play *Frosty* to delight her, or at least something upon that vein.

I let muscle memory take charge to flow with the first swipe, playing the beloved children's song about Rudolf. As I performed, I spotted that unnatural smile of the angel doll propped on a dirty, cloth napkin on a pulled out chair at the center of the dining room. It felt as though the little misfit's very presence decimated my reality.

Its reign of discontent in the happy resort had to end. I strode toward the center of the room to collect the doll to prevent what was sure to be many more poor performances, lackluster guest experiences, and even harsh reviews that were certain to come.

Yet the quick movement of a tall man in dark clothes drew my attention. Ben had arrived from the back entry, his crop in hand at his side. By his direction and speed, it appeared we were both going to descend upon the possessed doll. Perhaps that was the reason we both stopped and curiously watched each other.

I was unaware my music had ended until a toddler screeched, *"Rudolph!"* I turned to see the unruly child rush from her mother's lap, angrily wailing and bolting toward the large swinging door at the back where servers are always rushing through.

Ben dropped the crop, turned and raced into the path of the running toddler, lifting her before she reached the wide door. He carried the thrashing child, attempting to soothe her as she screamed about Rudolph.

Eyes were upon me. After all, I'd just caused a kid to have a meltdown because I couldn't deliver on Rudolph.

As quickly as I could manage, I packed up my violin and rushed out. I needed to get to my room and feel the joy of the beating heart of the resort. Somewhere away from that angel, whose presence brought this incident about.

I wasn't above cookies, though. They were a staple that I needed, especially in a time of crisis like this. I hardly slowed down in my detour to get to the kitchen, weaving past the sous chef and rapidly grabbing two snowman-shaped treats. Despite the detour, my speed had me to the hall of employee rooms in under seven minutes. I wasn't certain if that amount of time helped calm my nerves or if it was the joyful embrace of the spirits who'd returned to comfort me.

I strode through, my fingertips no longer buzzing, and I slowed at Ben's door that was slightly open with his light on. Maybe he'd headed straight to his room after being hit at by the enraged child. I stopped, feeling the urge to knock to make sure he wasn't bandaging any tiny scratches caused by my performance challenges.

If anything, I could deliver one of my cookies and give him the opportunity to vent about the angel. After years of knowing each other, people did that sort of thing.

I hugged my violin against my chest and tapped his door, which silently opened all the way in invitation. I stepped in, smiling in greeting, hoping it didn't come across the same way as the angel doll's awkward expression. But after entering, I didn't see Ben.

I scanned further inside the pristine room that contained minimal belongings. The only mess to be found was a mountain of red cards in his trash bin. Several others had already collapsed onto the floor.

I spun at the sound of a click from behind, only to find the door closed. Panicked, I rushed to it and took hold of the knob, twisting and jiggling it without success. This was a spectral prank that no spirit had ever used on me.

I sighed, focusing on the feel of my violin case against my chest. As if the situation couldn't get any worse, crumbles from the now-squished, warm cookie broke off onto his spotless hard floor. Now I'd invaded his privacy *and* made a mess.

I switched to hugging my violin with one arm and fisted the cookies as I wiggled his door with hope in compassion by any entity. Liora probably did this to force me to accept the bow. The expectant spirits wanted romance back on the top of the list. And understandable, given my recent failure.

I smeared the end of my sleeve on the floor to gather up the icing blob and rushed over, putting my instrument on the desk so I could stuff the cookie crumbles somewhere in the mound of cards. Curiously, I caught sight of my name on one.

Tessa, please

I wasn't certain why he would have thrown a card away after only two words. The words of more cards were easily visible.

Dear Tessa, I would like to give you

Dearest Tessa, this violin was my grandfather's.

He'd wanted to give me more than just a bow. But that seemed absurd, given we were nothing more than coworkers whose greetings were cordial at most. We weren't even friends. I couldn't accept a gift beyond something simple, especially not after the way I'd brought about the memory of his late grandfather.

On the other side of his desk, I saw one of the few possessions within sight. A wooden antique case that would house a violin. Something that must have been priceless to him.

I dusted crumbles into a gap between cards in the bin, spotting the words in another.

Tessa, Things haven't been the same here without you. I would love for you to accept this violin and use it for your upcoming performances.

And another.

Dearest Tessa, you are such a wonderful woman

If only that one had been complete. Would it have mentioned anything more than a violin? Maybe the way he'd looked at me earlier did mean something.

The door clicked behind me, startling me, but when I turned, no one was there. I wouldn't pass on the opportunity for freedom at the sight of the opening at the door. I swiftly took hold of my violin, then rushed to the door that easily opened the rest of the way, only to have me careening into the broad frame of the man who called this room his home.

Much to Say

Ben

I expected any number of things to occur in this lodge, but not to end up with Tessa in my arms. Not once, and definitely not twice. And again, she had this sort of panic as I supported her weight close to my chest.

The first time I'd held her had been a welcome shock. Then, I felt like I may have been turning into a pervert whose manhood got hard at a near grope of this woman. This time, though, she smelled like fresh-baked cookies, and I couldn't stop myself from breathing her in. For a moment, I could do nothing, which made me feel even more like a leering man that she would probably want to run from or file a sexual harassment complaint against. I quickly righted her to stand steadily on her own feet, stepping back to give her a respectful distance.

There was plenty I wanted to say to her. *Good to see you. Are you okay? That's just a tool I tucked in my pants because I would never have inappropriate thoughts about you.* And I was desperately trying not to have any unprofessional physical responses to this beautiful woman whose warm body I'd held against me for a second, slightly longer time.

Standing unmoving, she stared at me with an expression I couldn't make sense of. Maybe expectant. That gave me enough time to gather my thoughts about the oddness of her in my room.

"Right. You came to me for the bow," I said. It seemed a bit strange that she went in, not that I minded her in my room. I couldn't imagine anywhere else I wanted to be with her.

She shook her head slowly, looking at the crop where it currently sat lodged in my belt. Hopefully that was her interest, because I didn't want to think about the possibility that she was trying to process the thickening bulge that she might have felt.

Still holding tight to her violin, she stepped sideways past me into the hallway and signed her thanks to me. A blue streak of cookie icing stuck to her chin after the motion. It was no wonder that she smelled so sweet.

She swiftly went to her door before I could come up with any polite words. Then she glanced over at me while taking the knob at her door and opening it. It was one of those looks where something needs to be said, but isn't.

I gripped the handle of the crop, not wanting this encounter to wrap up in such a way. "I..."

She stopped, her attention returning to me. And then she nodded in question, awaiting whatever I had to say.

And there was so much I had to say. I squeezed the handle, twisting the crop at my side, causing her to look down at the nervous fidgeting. "Are you sure you didn't need something...anything at all?"

She grinned, though small, before lowering her violin to the floor with a globbed napkin that had a smashed cookie in it. When she rose, she pulled out her phone from her side pocket. She speedily typed and came over and handed it to me. More of the icing smear crusted the edges. *I just wanted to make sure you weren't hurt after the little girl went feral over Rudolf.*

I hadn't been bothered by the incident at all. I liked kids. "It was a nice break as opposed to seeing people celebrating Valentine's day year-round."

She was running her fingers through a tangle of icing in her hair when I handed her the phone. She nodded and typed again, turning the screen to me. *You're a sweet person. Thank you.*

Sweet. Was that a good word or a bad word? I could feel the walls tightening around me, suffocating me due to my own uncertainty. I knew this opportunity was slipping away from me, and I could feel the clamminess of my hand against the leather handle I twisted. I puffed out air before saying, "It was good talking to you, Tessa. Well, goodnight."

And it wasn't even nighttime. I stepped sideways to my door, offering her a quick nod before grabbing it and stepping inside.

"Good night? Good night?" I muttered the words low to myself, sinking against the door and scrubbing my face. I glanced over at the mess of cards that were equally riddled with nonsense. I had so much to say, yet no words to come up with.

Aloneness

Tessa

Whatever had remained of the cookies turned into a gooey clump in my fist. Worse, my tight embrace on my violin case felt as though it might shatter it. Loosening the hold, I went to my bed and laid the violin down before slumping onto the plush mattress.

How was it that a man who had so much to say had no words—not even in writing? He could speak to anyone else. Then again, I'd lost all ability to think for the short time he held me in his arms. That warmth was unlike anything I'd felt in my life. I couldn't even explain why the closeness to his body felt so good.

I knew why that riding crop seemed so pleasing, though. What I would give to have him use it on me for an entire evening and night. Neither one of us would find the words to end whatever might come of such an encounter. Then again, neither of us would be able to say what needed to be said to begin such an evening. Maybe I would have to be the one typing out my wants, hopeful he would be eager to fulfill them.

While pondering on the idea of passion with Ben, the warm and gooey sensation squeezing between my fingers took hold. Those cookies were no longer anything more than a mess in my tight fist. I went to the bathroom and tossed them in the trash before washing my hands to rid myself of the buttercream frosting. On to my music to coax me into calm.

I took out my violin and bow, relaxing myself and the spirits of the lodge to the call of Mozart. But that joy didn't last long before a saddening presence overcame me, causing another piercing cry from my violin.

How had that little angel doll entered my room? It was as though there would be no safety from it while I played my beloved music. And to haunt me further, all the warmth of the invisible life of the lodge dispersed, leaving me at the mercy of a depressed doll whose smile told nothing of joy.

I doubted it could read, but I got out my phone and typed, anyway.

Go away!

It was already gone when I looked its direction again. But that despair in the room didn't depart, it lingered. Playing my violin to relax myself would be useless, so I gave up on music, deciding instead on rest before an evening performance.

After turning off my lights, the moment I laid down and my head hit the pillow, I felt the movement on my bed. The little creature having drawn closer. I had the mind to grab it and take it straight to Mariah, so she could be rid of it. But, then again, maybe it had brought the abundance of Christmas and a different sort of joy. And I did love Christmas and the sight of the happy families.

I just didn't like this void of warmth from the spirits, who usually filled me with contentment. Especially while alone in my room.

Alone was fine. Alone involved no words, or rather, no lack of words.

Maybe this little specter was just alone, much like I'd felt most of my life. After all, the spirits that usually surrounded me had quite literally ghosted me due to its presence. And, somehow, this lonely little creature that oozed despair into the room was my only comfort for the moment.

Ruminations

Ben

It was an evening of groaning at my own actions. I was too flustered to even go anywhere near the lobby, most likely to end up looking like a lost puppy in the back of the room. And once I'd made it into my room, I ruminated even more, awaiting Tessa's music to trickle through the vents and walls.

How long had I been in love with her? Since day one around three years ago? Her dark brown hair was to mid-back at the time, and she would always comb her fingers through it, often letting long bangs curtain her eyes that were a magnificent hazel. It wasn't as though I could help my attraction to her back then. She'd always been the most remarkably beautiful woman I'd ever seen. And when she played, it only magnified her appeal, like an untouchable angel who'd traded her harp for a violin. But after she landed in my arms today and looked up at me with such breathlessness, it made me wish she was beneath me with the same look in her eyes.

I lay deathly still, haunted by a medley of mental visuals and driven mad from not hearing the melodious notes that always escaped her room at night, stuck between getting up and giving her the violin, but knowing it might make her even more standoffish. I wanted her closer, not more distanced.

I remained awake, contemplating how I would go in the morning and give it to her without looking like a desperate, love-sick puppy. But, unfortunately, well before 6 am, I was already receiving messages, but for water leaks and broken heaters along with the wine cellar door unbudging because a broomstick lodged it closed. It turned out a quarrelsome couple spent a night in there, but come morning they were magically happy. At least they wouldn't be leaving negative reviews.

I hadn't even found time to go in search of the angel or take the bow to Tessa. The moment I heard a violin playing Christmas music, I went straight to my room to retrieve the bow.

Just a gift for a friend, that's all it has to be. This wasn't weird. She would just see it as me being nice—unless she wanted to see it as more than that. She'd gone from a coworker I politely greeted upon seeing to someone I fantasized about far too much. And they were probably only meant to be fantasies, given she'd never shown interest.

After retrieving the bow, I strode to the dining area, to the tunes of Christmas music. But those musical pieces seemed unusually strained. I went in as the music ended, bow in one hand and crop in the other, quickly spotting Tessa seated. But her wide eyes toward the tree suggested more than discomfort. I knew all too well what caused such a sensation of unease. It was a sensation in the room, and that little possessed doll must have been lurking in the tree, tormenting her with its presence.

Not on my watch!

I strode quickly, scanning the magnificently adorned, tall Christmas tree, but I saw nothing. I stepped into the visual path of the tree, drawing her attention.

Her expression brightened, more beautiful than I'd seen ever before. Even if I could slightly sense the doll's presence, her warmth drowned out that emptiness it had a way of causing. I'd become drunk on her until she raised her bow.

I held up mine and went to where she sat with her violin pressed to her neck, still in position for the next piece.

I extended the bow to her. Right now, she needed to perform, and this had to help. "It's the angel doll. I'm going to find it and be rid of it."

I waited until she took the bow; her glancing up at me with what had to be silent appreciation. And those hazel eyes were damned near soul-melting as they held to mine.

As she played *White Christmas*, I strode the narrow path between tables of dining guests, headed towards the tree. The angel had been in there. It was the only explanation for her distraught expression.

While searching the tree, I peeked to watch her stepping with the same grace as she always had when she performed, even slightly smiling at the guests as she filled the room with warmth. If there was one thing I never appreciated before meeting her, it was Christmas, but something about the way she altered the world surrounding us was simply enamoring. And now, the way the neckline of her black dress scooped to just the right amount and she would sway had me salivating.

When the number ended, and she straightened, her hazel eyes shifted to me in a stare that forced me to busy myself with a search of the tree. I would have sensed the creature's heightened play on my emotions if it was this close, though.

Oh, Christmas Tree filled the air, but in an enchanting call I longed to answer. I shouldn't embarrass myself by drooling over this woman coming nearer. Instead, I plunged the crop into the limbs and pushed the silver garland downward, pretending to search for the possessed angel and circling around the behemoth tree. That only allowed for me to have a better view of her in the form-fitting dress she wore.

Restorations

Tessa

Even if Ben kept his distance, I knew now that he was as attracted to me as I was to him. I saw it in his eyes. I felt it. In the absence of the spirits of the resort, I now sensed something too enrapturing for known words to express.

Those sensations made accepting the bow no easier for me, though. I didn't want to take something special from him, certainly not an antique that was valued at possibly a thousand dollars. He would've sold it if it meant nothing.

I also didn't want for him to believe me indifferent. I wanted this chance to get to know him, so I accepted it, and the priceless gift slid over the strings as smooth as silk, letting the most ordinary of Christmas melodies seem magical. Enjoyable to play, even if not the romantic pieces I would normally have chosen.

Once my performance was over, I needed to thank him. I also needed to discover how the angel doll affected his emotions. He'd planned to capture it, but that might end this joy of Christmas that had spread. It would cause an innocent creature to suffer loneliness if trapped away somewhere. The doll hadn't stopped my elation at the sight of Ben, so that had to prove something in its favor.

At my long afternoon break, I gathered my coat and gloves and secured a strap to my case so I could sling it across my chest to hang at my side. I couldn't dare to part with it. Not even briefly. I went outside, hoping I might *happen* to bump into Ben.

At the side courtyard, the sounds of children's music danced over the sparse flurries of snow. Not like the sounds from a radio or children's toy, but like at the carnivals. Like a carousel. We had one on property that probably hadn't operated in decades. It was considered historic and close to the conifer forest that guests sometimes hiked.

I had to admit to glee when I walked out to where I could see the moderately small carousel, now operational with children atop the painted horses and a couple seated on the sleigh. And Ben operating it, much to the enjoyment of the families.

Every step his way caused the tips of my gloved fingers to tingle. From anticipation at first, then from knowing that I should have something typed out to say to him, then me digging in my pocket and the realization that I'd been so absent-minded while I readied myself to see him that I forgot my phone.

Now I began to realize why I rarely went outside, preferring the ability to escape interaction and being blanketed by the spectral warmth inside the lodge. Out here I was exposed.

I stopped, staring at the scene before me through the fog of my tense sigh. I still had time to turn around—He turned his head, scanning the surroundings. His attention quickly landed on me, though, and I lost all ability to function under his gaze. Was I leaving or staying? I didn't know anymore. I only knew I longed to go to him.

"Tessa," he called, beaming and swatting the crop's flap on the thin blanket of powdery snow.

That beam gave me the courage to take those final steps in his direction. In truth, each one felt like an eternity, but his smile pulled me forward. Once I finally stopped in front of him, I tapped my fingertips on my chin, and then pointed down to my violin case resting by my side.

"No problem," he replied. "I'm glad it helped."

I supposed it did, but not in the way he expected. He had been what I found so uplifting. Even when stripped of the warmth that had always surrounded me, his presence unleashed an inferno far more powerful than anything else I'd ever felt. I wanted that feeling to remain more than anything supernatural that only fueled contentment.

He glanced back at the ride he'd always kept clean just for show, but there had never been reason to get it running until the recent influx of families who came for the Christmas experience that seemed to be spreading word of festive joy online like wildfire.

Most likely due to a little angel whose power I could make no sense of yet. I simply knew I didn't want it to suffer loneliness.

A Little Help

Ben

I wanted to melt into the snow beneath me when I saw Tessa. Even my gloved hand ached from the tightness of my grip, and I forced myself to relax, not wanting to draw attention to my reaction.

She combed her fingers through her hair and nodded her chin to the carousel, slightly smiling, before glancing at me.

I was more than a little jealous of how she so easily conversed without words spoken. The thought made me more desperate to know what she would say to me if given the chance to talk my ear off. They would be beautiful words, no doubt, but still didn't compare to how much I loved her expressions and music that so perfectly conveyed her emotions.

I shrugged and swatted the leather flap of the crop at the powdery snow between us, hoping to keep my jumbling words flowing. "Seemed like a good time to put the engineering degree to use."

She kicked the toe of her shiny black boot to the leather flap, her beaming smile even larger to question me about it.

"Oh, you know," I answered, sighing from the frustration. "Catching that creepy doll."

The music accompanying the carousel slowed as the ride came to an end after the set timer wrapped up. I reached forward and pushed the old button again, keeping it in motion for another few minutes.

Her gloved hand rubbed against mine as she gripped the lower part of the leather handle of the crop.

I felt naked releasing it, but I wouldn't refuse her request to hold it. And I didn't know what to think when she swatted the back of my knee with it. Not hard, but still surprising.

Now her long bangs fell forward to curtain those expressive eyes that were lined to perfection. Dear god did I find it hard to stand so close to her while she bore such an innocent yet alluring expression. And she was jesting, something that, to my knowledge, she didn't do with anyone.

My attempt at a swallow caught in my throat. What was she saying? Perhaps when she cocked her head slightly, it was a question.

"I knocked the doll down with it a few times, but he's still gotten away once out of sight."

She nodded, shrugging in interest, somewhat melancholy.

"It affects you, too." I nodded, glancing back to the ride that slowed a bit too early. That repair job hadn't lasted long. "Looks like this show is over," I said to her before telling the disappointed riders that the carousel had stopped working.

Luckily, she didn't leave while I saw to the families getting off safely. She simply held the crop with the leather flap in front of her, inspecting it. It wouldn't hurt to see if she might help in capturing the possessed angel doll.

I returned to her. "If you're interested, we could..."

She cocked her head from where the flap blocked her face from view.

"I've been needing someone to help use that."

Her brow raised from behind a veil of bangs.

"To swat it down so I can catch it. You know, if you want during your break, I could use a little help." I grabbed at my side for the coaxing handle of the crop that was no longer there.

She handed it to me and then raised her hand and tapped her wrist before spreading her gloved fingers of both hands to extend six fingers.

It was at least a few hours until six p.m. I hadn't received a call to do anything in particular aside from my usual duties, so I might have some time. The doll did seem to affect her more than other people, so much she'd been aware of it a few times. Even almost captured it yesterday.

She motioned to herself, then to me, suggesting I lead the way.

"Sure thing." I went over to my small pack that had part of my sack lunch remaining. "Are you hungry?" I pulled the brown bag out. "I know you like the cookies with buttercream frosting."

At that, she beamed.

We both did.

A Kiss

Tessa

I'd not eaten since breakfast, so the thought of buttercream icing had my mouth watering. And when he dug into the paper bag and retrieved the clear plastic wrapper that had the fresh snowman inside, my stomach started doing flips.

"We can head to storage to get some extra supplies to catch it." He waited until I had the wrapper off the cookie before leading me to the gravel path, avoiding tromping over the glistening snow so it remained picture perfect, though that might not last long given a high-pitched voice from behind mentioned snow-balls.

After breaking the cookie in half, I held a piece out for him to take. But he refused.

"I know buttercream frosting is your favorite flavor. I would have saved it for you anyway," he said, moving at the pace of a relaxing stroll, but keeping his attention ahead.

It was a gesture I found to make him even more endearing.

"I'd hoped to catch it before you returned," he said, heading toward a large shed close to the lodge at the end of the path.

I took a small bite that left my snow-man headless, letting the buttercream melt in my mouth. I felt a bit guilty going along with this goal of his to trap the angel doll. Despite those feelings of sorrow it had made me feel, when it came to Ben, things changed, even when in the doll's presence. And that seemed to brighten the room. As though my elation came out in my notes, spreading the refreshing warmth I felt. I couldn't let the little creature suffer loneliness, but I also needed to figure out more about it and make sure Ben didn't hunt it without me.

I came closer to him and bumped his shoulder, shrugging in question. I liked this ability of his to understand me without the need of a phone. Hopefully, it could continue and not get awkward.

The tall man glanced over, uncertainty evident in his expression before he looked ahead. "I just didn't like the idea of it, you know...upsetting you." He waved the crop in front of him. "Once we get somewhere warm, I can show you how this works."

I laughed. And not just a low one. It resonated, causing him to side-eye me.

"What?" he asked sheepishly. "It has a bit of a learning curve."

And I wanted to experience that learning curve he mentioned. I had no idea what expression I made that caused him to be flustered and look ahead to the storage shed. And soon enough, I finished my cookie, and we were there, with him opening the door for me.

Once inside the warm building, I removed my violin, gloves, and jacket, fairly certain my movement in my form-fitting dress received his interest from my periphery. When I looked at him, though, he turned and led me around a shelf that had gardening supplies. I had no idea how this man had the time to ensure the cleanliness of this place, but it was almost as spotless as his room.

"Let's see here," he said, scanning the shelves. "Something for a trap." He handed me the crop to hold. "Would you kindly hold this?"

I took it from him, swinging it side to side as he turned and reached to the back of a shelf that was shoulder height, pulling out a scarlet coil of rope that still had ties around it. "I can make a small net out of this, so if the angel gets knocked down, the netting can hold it before it gets up." He pulled another coil down with the same new texture and ties on it. And it wasn't rope to be used outdoors, this was a rope for binding.

And heat most certainly filled me at the sight of him with that type of rope.

As he unwound the red rope without looking at it, he jutted his chin to my hand. "Maybe you can practice with that while I do this." I didn't know I was staring at him with an odd expression, until he added, "The doll's possessed. It won't hurt."

I nodded, biting my lower lip so not to smile. Nope, maybe not hurt the doll, but definitely designed for a physical response in people. He put down the rope, turned, and reached upward, allowing me the perfect opportunity to lightly swat the back of his thigh with the crop.

A roll of paper towels fell as he turned to me with surprise.

I only shrugged at his questioning glance. And at least it turned into a smile. "It's usually perched high."

He picked up the roll of paper towels and set them on the edge of a tall shelf, saying, "Most of the times it's somewhere easy to spot around this high."

He leaned against the wall, picked up the rope and looped it in an oddly simple way, netting it.

Now I had to wonder if he knew how to use it and was acting naïve. Perhaps he was attempting to gather whether I knew anything about shibari. He continued to weave the rope, which I couldn't help but notice just how skilled he was. "Fishing net," he said to me. "Me and..." he paused, looking down as he knotted more rope and stretched it. "I used to go fishing a lot."

Well, at least that explained his skill with those ropes. But the slight pause showed a bit of sadness as he worked. I could only assume this brought back the memory of his late grandfather. But that shift in his emotions didn't last for long.

"You think you can use that crop to knock that roll of paper towels down?" he asked, jutting his chin upward.

I nodded and glanced upward to the roll that was far too high for me to reach, even with the crop. I swiped, only managing to tap the shelf.

"Not quite like that." He put the rope down on the shelf and extended his hand to me. "May I?"

I nodded and gave him the crop, a little taken aback when he circled around behind me with it. When I turned my head to look over my shoulder, he was coming to stand close to my back.

My stomach fluttered with nerves from the closeness. I'd thought this man handsome since the first day I saw him. Now he'd come to be behind me with a whip I was fairly certain he believed was only for horses and angels—and not a woman dressed like a naughty angel for Christmas.

He reached around me to place the warm grip on my open hand. Of course my chest quivered. Most men didn't care to be this close to me once they knew I couldn't speak. The few that ignored that fact quickly changed their minds after much time with me. I didn't bother trying anymore. Until now.

He had me raise the crop high into the air as he spoke close to my ear. "I promise we'll catch it, so everything gets back to normal for you."

But I didn't want everything back to normal—I wanted this. This closeness. This man whose body I sank back against, both hopeful and fearful of what might happen next.

He went rigid behind me, his hand wrapped over mine on the handle of the crop, lifted upward toward the paper towels. I could feel the warmth of his breath on my shoulder. This sensation both heated me and resulted in a shiver that had nothing to do with the temperature. For far too long, we stood like that; me waiting and him unmoving save for his chest that swelled against my back.

And then a firmness in his pants.

My swallow was loud in my throat. As was his.

"I..." warm air from a quivering breath rolled against my neck as I tilted my head to the side. Everything within me hoped for something from him. Anything at all to move this in a direction I wanted to go, but feared to be the one to take the lead.

Only more heated breaths rolled down onto my neck and shoulder. That swollen girth remained, but didn't move.

"I..." he seemed to be lost for words yet again, but his tone suggested a discomfort with the situation. The crop lowered as he no longer supported the hold on it.

I turned my head to peer upward over my shoulder at his mesmerizing brown eyes, only to find a distraught expression as he rubbed his lips together.

A buzzing came from his belt, but he ignored it.

"I..." His third attempt to speak ended on a sigh.

Another buzz came from his belt. Again, he ignored it. There was this lightened weight in the air.

His lips flattened into a line that expressed agitation at the interruption.

His phone rang, causing him to sigh and reach for it. His jaw clenched when he looked at it. "I have to take this," he said before backing away and lifting the phone to his ear. "Yeah?"

I remained in place but looked ahead, my back only inches in front of him, though it had become awkward hearing a muffled voice of a woman coming through.

"I'll be there soon..." he groaned as he stepped further backward. "I have to go out to help with a cart someone decided to take into the forest." He stepped around me and took the partially netted rope from the shelf. "I'll help you with your coat." He walked me around to the door, lifting my coat and holding it open for me to slide my arms in the sleeves.

I put on my gloves and strapped my violin over my shoulder, and he opened the door for me, sending in a chilly breeze with flurries of snow.

"I'll walk you to the side entry, " he said, before a silent walk to a private employee entrance of the lodge. After opening it and stepping me in, he said, "See you later, Tessa." He looked at me in that way I'd quickly grown to love.

Since no one currently walked this narrow corridor, it wouldn't hurt to see how he responded to me coming closer. I stepped forward; unprofessionally close. When he didn't distance himself, I raised onto the balls of my feet and, refusing my own inhibition, pressed my lips to his.

What may have only been seconds dragged by while I awaited his response—anything at all. Be it to wrap his arms around me or simply brushing his tongue against mine. But that didn't happen. When I was about to lower to my normal height, his mouth finally moved in reciprocation, his tongue meeting mine. Though only brief before he pulled away, we'd shared a kiss that would make the most explosive fireworks jealous.

"Thank you, Tessa," he said in haste. "I hope to see you again." He took only one more second to study me before turning and leaving.

A Simple Retrieval

Ben

Thank you? Thank you! A beautiful woman I've been in love with for years kisses me, and I say thank you. Not that it was much worse than when I said I hoped to see her again. As if we might not ever see each other again, even though she lives in the room next to mine.

She was so nice and wonderful. Kissing her felt perfect. But I shuddered to think about what it must be like to kiss me. While I also desperately needed to try again. To kiss her the right way, not like some adolescent boy behind the junior high school music building.

Everything that had occurred indicated she liked me to some extent. And now, I didn't know what bothered me more, my inability to tell Tessa how I felt about her or whoever lodged a golf cart in the forest. Not that it mattered, I just needed to help get it out from between the trees and back on its wheels.

Two seasonal-hire teenagers were at the cart that had become stuck between a tree and a boulder. Once we'd righted the cart, both of them sat on the seat, not bothering to acknowledge the dirty clothes on the ground.

Thank god I had the crop with me out here. I used the end to scoop up what looked to be a shirt and a few pairs of undergarments and tossed them one by one onto the back seat of the cart.

The shorter of the two teens leaned against the wheel and started it. "There's a whole kit for you that spilled out." He pointed to the tree. "Just on the other side."

I didn't need to deal with anything else. I needed to get back to Tessa before the evening performance began. Cleanup was what those seasonal employees were supposed to help with, but they already backed the cart up and rode it down the walking path in reverse.

I went around the tree, finding a large, black case with contents that were obviously of sexual nature spilled out. Not that I was a prude, but a man who isn't having sex doesn't need to bother with researching sex stuff. But now—Now nothing! I just needed to get back and find her. Hopefully make sure I hadn't behaved in a way that seemed dismissive.

I was just fine with using my boot to kick whatever the heck these people got off on, which seemed to include some sort of long, furry black tail. But when a loosened coil of black rope caught my eye, I used the crop to lift it. And it happened to be similar to the smooth rope I'd been making a net of earlier.

My thoughts went to the surprise Tessa expressed when she'd seen my rope. I could have hoped I made an assumption about her response until I saw the end of a stick with a pink flap at the tip. It may have been pink, but it bore a striking similarity to the riding crop I carried. I used mine and knocked the item from beneath the spread suitcase.

I loathed the sight. If it had been black and a little longer, it would look like mine.

And, to my shame, Tessa seemed questioning about my crop. Everyone looked at it funny, actually. I leaned against the tree, my gaze unfocused on anything as I tried to remember the exact expressions on her face at the sight of it. But then I got lost in the memory of holding her against me. Pulled into the way she'd aroused me like no woman in my life had.

What if she was into a lifestyle I knew nothing about? But that would mean she wanted someone to hurt her. I couldn't do that. I wouldn't hurt her. Not a chance in hell would I let her be hurt.

After cramming the contents in the case, to which part of the tail hung out, I forced it shut. If I thought the oddities inside were disturbing, the image of a nude man with ropes wound around him imprinted on the leather made this all the creepier. This trip was supposed to be a quick job to retrieve a tipped golf cart, yet this was what I got stuck with.

I lifted the case off a blanket of pine needles, spotting a yellow pamphlet with an image of ropes around wrists. The bold lettering said *Shibari Knotwork*.

I picked it up, studying its front image for a moment. Making me feel even more like an idiot for the crop and the rope I'd nonchalantly carried about.

When I made it back to the main grounds, families played in the snow-covered yard, and I couldn't risk exposing children to the vulgar image. I wound up taking an extra hour walking through the trees to the employee entrance.

I just needed to get it to my room for now and cover it with a bunch of blankets. Then I could take it to the lost and found after the lobby empties for the night. Once inside, I took my jacket off and placed it over the side of the suitcase, hiding the most obscene part of the image. And I made my speedy retreat into the employee hall, sighing with relief that I'd managed to keep this unseen by coworkers and guests.

I was only steps from my door when Tessa exited her room with her violin in hand. When she saw me, she immediately smiled. It was heart-melting and meant for me. The force of the day and all the joys and disturbances slammed against me. I wanted to be with her. I needed to say something to her. To respond with my own smile.

To get rid of this case of obscene items I carried.

"Tessa..." I attempted to readjust and make certain the jacket didn't fall.

She pointed down the hall toward the door that led to the main area of the lodge and motioned to her mouth like food. This had been so imperfectly timed.

"Maybe after you're done..." I feared my hand couldn't grip the case tight enough.

She took out her phone and typed. *Do you want to eat with me?*

I desperately craved to be with her, yet I needed to get rid of this case. "I...need a shower." I reached my free hand for the handle of the crop out of habit, forgetting I had the small pamphlet tightly rolled in that fist. It fell to the floor. I stepped on it to hide it, but she'd already looked downward with puzzlement. It seemed as if the world wanted to cruelly torture me, because, on top of everything else, the jacket slowly slipped downward.

Tessa leaned over and reached for it to keep it from falling, but I tried to multitask my hold and managed to still it.

If not for what I carried, this would have been that perfect moment of closeness. The one where I should have said something. Had courage. Anything. Instead, I was sweating and unsteady. I needed to get to my room before I said something to further make me look silly.

"I'll find you." I kept a hold on the jacket to hide the case and turned to my door, forcing it open and stepping in. I didn't mean to slam the door on her before tossing the case down on the floor close to my entry. I tried to catch my breath, glaring at the obscene container of sex toys. My chance to no longer look like that school boy failed. Now, far worse, I looked like I outright rejected her.

No Crop Required

Tessa

Ben's quick departure to his room didn't upset me. I'd grown to understand how he behaved when nervous. And, from what I'd seen from his interactions with others, this only happened with me. He cared about me. No matter how poorly he worded it, I understood it.

After that kiss we shared, I felt as though my life had changed. Joy blanketed me and remained to keep me warm and cozy. Even when I played in my room. I sensed that angel, but it wasn't as painful. Sure, there were still feelings, but not the despair I'd felt upon my return. Overall, it felt like elation. Like the curse of that angel made these interactions with Ben possible and had made this season wonderful. If this continued, I would be on track to perform successfully, with or without the presence of the spirits of the lodge.

But that depended on what Ben wanted. No matter how much I liked him or how marvelous his responding kiss was, how long would his interest in me last? And could I bear it if he changed his mind as the other few men had?

But those worries wouldn't help me play my violin. Ben was different. I needed to remember that. Hope for more time with him was why I had no fear as I now wove through the dinner crowd. It was why playing seasonal music instead of the repeated instances of love songs didn't bother me.

I began this performance with *White Christmas*, playing it with precision. Not a drop of misery leeched into the notes.

And the performance improved as I continued, choosing festive pieces that were both romantic and peaceful. Even able to walk around in the crowded banquet room with the slower pieces I played.

Soon, Ben came to stand at the back of the room. He arrived dressed casually in a black sweater and jeans, which was even nicer than the relaxed but on-call attire I almost always saw him in.

My heart fluttered with whatever elation the possessed angel allowed to be set free. The little specter was near, but spreading joy. Every song filled the room with the endorphins equally powerful as those expected upon entry into this magical match-making resort. And once I'd performed for well over an hour, I bowed, ready to call it an evening, since there wasn't any private party scheduled for later.

After packing my instrument, I made my way to where Ben waited at the grand doors of the room. Just as the bow could so gracefully create melody with its glide over the strings, my feet seemed to do the same with the steps his way, creating this blissful internal flow that reached into every cell in my body. And the closer to him I came, the more enrapturing the feeling.

His hands were hidden behind his back. "Sorry about earlier," he said. He then presented a snow-man shaped cookie to me, part of it wrapped in a napkin. "I snagged one of these fresh for you." When I took the cookie, he scratched his neck, looking around anxiously before returning his attention to me. "How about we go somewhere and try to catch that little doll?"

I nodded and pulled out my phone and asked, *the netting?*

"Yeah, about that," he said, reaching to his side where he'd usually had the crop tucked in his work belt. But he didn't have the belt or the crop.

I motioned to his side and flicked my wrist in the way one would swat with the crop.

"And that." He made a soured expression. "We can just..." he sighed and placed his hands on his hips, his pitch increasing. "Do you know what all of those things are used for?"

I didn't know *all* the things they were used for, but I knew of plenty. And my giggle said so, but I attempted to hide it behind the cookie I bit into.

"So you do," he responded, then let out a disappointed sigh. "I'm such a..."

I shook my head and placed a hand to his chest, hushing him from self-deprecation or embarrassment. I had to take another bite of cookie and tuck it in my mouth and get out my phone to fully respond. *You're perfect.* I hoped it wasn't too bold.

"Perfectly silly," he replied. "Anyway, we can just walk around and you can play somewhere where there's not much furniture and has a bare floor."

I typed. *Like our rooms?* When I turned the screen to him, he flashed another one of those unnerved expressions. One that could almost appear as being repulsed by the thought of being in a room with me. But I knew otherwise now.

"Just like walk the halls or something and you play violin. I'll catch it while it's slumped on the floor. No crop required." He turned and headed toward the lobby of the lodge, but as soon as he stepped out, his phone buzzed at his hip.

He got it out and read a text. "Families are asking if the carousel is fixed yet." He turned to me with disappointment. "Maybe later?"

I typed. *I can go with you, if you want.* I turned the screen to him.

His attention went to the phone. "Sure. We should probably get our coats, though."

A Bridge Broken

Ben

Once outside with an LED lamp in my hand for moderate illumination, Tessa speedily came to my side. I strode with slightly slower steps than usual so that she could leisurely keep up.

Everything that had been building between us felt like a fight between flames and ice. I wanted her. But I might not be enough if she preferred a man who knew how to use that crop and ropes. Those thoughts plagued me as we walked in the cold, dark evening, more flurries of snow than earlier falling between us.

"We'll get back to capturing that angel after this," I said. "It shouldn't take too long."

We arrived at the carousel that was now decked out with garland and large crimson bows. With her on my heels, I stepped up onto the ride and helped her up as well. I lowered in front of the maintenance box and opened it up, examining the wiring.

Then music came from behind me. Her playing, *Santa, Baby*. I liked the flirtatious and peppy tune, listening as I examined the cogs. Not a thing in the world appeared wrong with the carousel. Most likely, as with almost everything, this was Liora or another specter's doing. And that meant this would be closed to guests in order for them to return to their rooms to later be snugly trapped inside. It was just like those spirits to press for love and elation.

"Looks like Liora doesn't want anyone having this sort of fun after dark." Once Tessa finished her number, I shut the engine box and stood and turned to her, stretching my back before leaning against the center wall and studying her seated on one of the black horses that had a red bow around its neck. "Once we get that angel, you can play your preferred romance pieces."

She lowered her instrument and took out her phone. *I like Christmas music. Besides, maybe the angel isn't as bad as we thought.* She added a shrug, feigning indifference for how it had attempted to shred her world apart.

"I'm not so sure about that," I replied. "I guess we just need to check indoors again to see."

Her mouth slightly opened as though she had something to say, and even though I knew she wouldn't speak, that heart-melting look in her eyes had returned and said so many words. She held onto the pole and descended on my side of the horse.

I decided it was best that we go in as quickly as possible to get this angel hunt on track again, given the carousel would operate whenever a spirit decided it would be best. But when I was at the tail of the horse, the carousel lurched with a speed that had me grabbing for the wooden seat, and to protect Tessa, who'd clung to the pole.

My effort to ensure she didn't fall caused me to reach and pull her to me, balancing both of us against the wooden horse. It was another one of those moments where events unfolded to land her close to me. And another moment that the short amount of time caused a stirring that went deep into my soul—and pants.

Those sensations abounded until I felt the prod of her violin between us. Surely I hadn't damaged her beloved instrument in an attempt to keep her safe. Another flash of lights and lurch of the heavy machinery made my backing away ineffective, and the violin at least partially smashed between us. This time, I stepped back and gripped the hard tail of the horse to ensure I didn't further land against her.

"I...I'm so sorry." I looked down to the violin she lifted. "I didn't even think to make sure the carousel wouldn't start up again with a test run. I'll examine your violin for you."

She turned to leave. At least I thought she planned to leave as quickly as possible, but she went to sit on a sleigh on the now-stilled and dark carousel.

I went to get the lantern and then to sit beside her, waiting for her examination of the instrument to be complete. She fidgeted with the tuners, then down to the bridge—the most delicate piece.

She then passed it over to me to examine it, pointing to the warped bridge.

"Tessa..." I said, sighing heavily. I couldn't bear seeing her so distraught, especially because of my actions.

She gripped my hand, at least pretending this was fine. But it wasn't fine. Nothing about this was fine.

"I have a violin in my room," I said, trying to read whether she would be hesitant to accept it. "I can attempt to fix yours if you only want to borrow mine."

A Little Weird

Tessa

It was a relatively inexpensive violin. Nothing that I couldn't have repaired, and I could rent one from a nearby shop in the morning. But to Ben, this was so much more. He worried too much. I couldn't even fathom why someone so competent and charming as him became so flustered.

I pulled out my phone and typed, *We can go to your room*. I had no desire to accept a highly valued antique violin, though. I wanted to be alone with Ben, to have him all to myself without any worry between us.

His heavily shadowed face relaxed, causing the tension to ease from my own shoulders. He extended his gloved hand to mine, gently assisting me down from the carousel. Once we were on our way, both of us seemed eager to get to his room, keeping a quick pace as we hurried through the chilly night air.

By the time we reached the employee quarters, we were both out of breath. And we still didn't slow down until we were in front of his door. At the sight of crumpled yellow paper lying on the floor, I bent down to pick it up and smoothed out the creases, seeing that this had to do with Shibari knotwork. An amused smile played on my lips when I glanced at Ben.

"That's um—not mine," he blurted. He took the paper from me and tucked it in his pocket. "I'll just see to its safe arrival to the lost and found tomorrow."

I found nothing wrong with the brochure. It was something I held curiosity in learning more about. I stepped forward between him and his door, raising onto my toes to kiss him. This time, he kissed me without hesitation, wrapping his arm around my lower back. And this was far more intense than before. More passionate. Him pouring his soul into the heat of the moment, even opening the door and walking me backward into his room, continuing the scorching make-out session all the way until after his door closed, and we had no concern of being seen.

He used his hold on my back to lower me onto his bed before taking my instrument case and turning to place my violin and the case on his desk. And that gave me a full view of luggage with an artful image of someone nude covered in bindings. And, interestingly, a furry tail stuck out, not real—hopefully.

The sudden stillness from Ben's direction caught my attention, causing me to shift my gaze back to his silly expression.

"It's not what you think," he said. "I'm not weird. Well, I am a little, but not like that."

I never suggested he was weird, nor did I believe he'd been using whatever hid in that interesting case. But I did raise a brow in good teasing humor.

"Not that I think anything is wrong with it—that sort—" a quick sigh escaped him. "This looks bad, but it's going straight to the lost and found after I cover it in the morning. Can't let kids be exposed to that." His attention went between me and the case. He yanked off his jacket and threw it on the container, hiding the visual of the roped man. This serious was one that I liked, though, as opposed to the worry from earlier.

I removed my coat, taking a moment to fold it neatly before setting it aside. Then, I perched on the edge of his bed and, teasingly slowly, unlaced my boots. While taking my time, I stole glances at him as I awaited what he would do next.

He responded by kicking off his boots with urgency and coming over to me, bending down, cupping my cheeks and kissing me, guiding me downward to lie on his bed and look up to him in all his scrumptious glory. There was even a flash of a dimple with his contained smile before his black sweater swallowed up his face as he worked it up and off, revealing a lean stomach that belonged on the cover of a magazine. My Joseph Gordon-Levitt, but far more handsome.

Next, it was my turn to remove my dress and toss it to the side, remaining on my back on the bed as he took in the sight of my white lace bralette and warm black leggings. Once again, he came to be on top of me, and my legs curled around his waist as he staked his claim over my mouth.

This wasn't like those times with someone selfish who only wanted my clothes off and got their quick sex. This was Ben, the sweet man who I had been attracted to for years. He didn't rush into a good fuck, even though it felt like his pants housed a massive wrench.

When he did pause to brace his elbows on either side of my head and looked down at me, I had no clue what to make of his expression, but it involved deep thought.

Unveiled

Ben

This was happening. We were happening. Me and Tessa. I was about to make love to the most beautiful, most talented and perfect woman to ever have walked this earth. And her entrancing hazel eyes demanded action from me.

But, in truth, I hadn't proven anything to her. No matter how hard my cock was, I hadn't even earned her. That angel still roamed. It could interrupt at any moment and ruin the very act of sex.

Her expression was quick to sour as I studied her. This would only work if she was happy, not because a specter did things like lock doors or cause me to break her violin.

The thought of what brought this to occur returned. I'd destroyed her beloved instrument. Her livelihood.

I quickly rose from atop her and went to the antique violin I wanted her to have, lifting it and taking it to her to open. "I want you to have this, Tessa."

She sat upright, absolutely stunning in her white lace bra. As she opened the case, I went to her instrument, opening it to retrieve the bow so she could play.

"We should try to catch the angel, so you're happy again." I held the bow in front of her puzzled face. She seemed almost hesitant when she took it and placed it on her lap. She motioned a phone near her ear and pointed to her coat.

I quickly retrieved her phone from the pocket and brought it to her.

She typed and then turned the screen to me. *I am happy with you.*

But that wasn't true. Circumstances made this good for her. I wouldn't exploit that.

"Tessa," I said, shaking my head. "Really and truly happy. That angel would gladly ruin what we have. I don't want that." I couldn't bear the thought of that happening.

Her eyes narrowed, and she typed and turned the screen. *Lay on the bed.* She stood with the violin and bow in hand, serious as she pointed to the bed.

"Tessa," I said as she went to the desk to lay down the instrument and case. The crop I'd used still lay on my desktop and she grabbed it, swiftly turning and pointing the flap at me, then toward the bed.

By her stern glare, she wasn't playing around in this demand of me.

I sat on the edge of the mattress, but she pointed downward toward the bed again. And I obeyed that stern order, laying in the middle of the bed and awaiting whatever she had in mind.

Without delay, she went and retrieved the violin and bow; her stare serious as she drew the bow upon the strings. Bach took hold of the room. I'd always loved it when she chose that one, even when a wall separated us late at night. She shut off the light, darkening the room to near blackness, and came over to the bed, still playing the number without need for illumination.

Suddenly, it felt as though the calm within the room dissipated, leaving me only with too many feelings to describe, joyful, euphoric. And Tessa, I felt her in a more powerful way than any time prior. Even the sounds coming from her violin felt crisp, not Christmas tunes, but something she often loved to play.

A lightweight object plopped beside me, and I knew what it was. *That damned angel.* I grabbed it and jumped upright in the dark, making sure I wasn't going anywhere near Tessa when I rushed to turn on the overhead light.

For once, I held the little creature that had caused so much trouble. I would be damned if it got away.

The piece by Bach ended on a screech, and Tessa lowered the violin and bow on the desk before extending an expectant hand to me.

"I just caught it. We have to get rid of it," I said to her, but she had no desire to listen to a word I had to say.

She grabbed the crop again, coming my way and swatting my thigh. I was thankful I hadn't removed my pants because that stung. She motioned again for me to give it to her, now closer.

What was the worst that could happen if she let it escape? We could look for it again later. For whatever reason unknown to me, it hadn't bothered her in here, so we could catch it when she finished her music tonight.

I handed her the doll, which she held with gentleness. As though she could simply ignore the misery it caused. She even went so far as to cradle the little monstrosity, caught in some sort of spell.

She made a silly face at me, waving her full hands forward in a silly way meant to be spooky, gesturing to all around us.

"Liora?" I asked.

Half of Tessa's mouth raised in a smile. She pushed as though with the power to be rid of something heavy, sending it in the distance.

"She leaves?" I was still puzzled and had no idea what this had to do with the doll Tessa currently snuggled close to her chest. But then she dropped the crop to the floor and came close to me, pointing in the direction she'd cast the imaginary spectral presence before raising the doll between us, placing her open palm onto my chest and then hers.

When I didn't respond, she repeated the movements, making evident that the angel somehow brought us together. Pushing away again at the imaginary Liora and shaking her head.

I crossed my arms, doubtful of her claim. "You're saying Liora has kept us apart, but the angel brings us together."

She nodded before going to the bed to her phone, still clinging to the possessed doll as she typed. She turned it to me. *Liora keeps us content alone. This angel makes her leave so we can experience how we truly feel.*

But that made no sense. "Liora makes people fall in love."

She typed again before turning the phone to me. *How long does that love last outside of this resort?*

I supposed plenty of people came back time and again to rekindle the flame they shared. I lowered my arms from my chest, having no further argument against what Tessa had to say. Thinking back to the waves of emotions lately, how sometimes even its presence couldn't dampen my joy in Tessa's company. I had no excuse to accept her words as anything other than truth.

Her attention remained on me as she set the doll on the desk before swiftly coming to stand against me and curl an arm around my neck as she planted a claiming kiss on my mouth.

How I loved the taste of buttercream icing that still slightly lingered. I didn't waste a moment unfastening my pants and pushing them and my boxers down and off, followed by tugging her leggings and underwear downward. Removing her bra as well, before leading her to the bed, not letting our bodies part as I laid her down. This would be a night we never forget.

Sugary Sweet

Tessa

It was true that spirits were mischievous creatures. Especially this one that managed to possess an angel doll. And over the days following that led to Christmas, more and more festive joy began to blossom. Whether love occurred with guests hungry for a partner, I wouldn't know, since the atmosphere was a winter wonderland that brought in families.

I played my favorites, both Christmas, classic, and modern. All sprinkled with a sugary, sweet magic more delectable than buttercream frosting. But come my Christmas eve performance, around midnight, I sensed the departure of the possessed angel. As though he'd found peace. He'd certainly made the holiday unbelievably joyful.

Soon after, when my performance ended, Ben strode over while I sealed the antique violin in its case. He was absolutely gorgeous, with his dark hair slightly mussed and that soft smile I loved since the first time I saw him. Unfortunately, he'd gotten rid of the crop that had excited me so.

He took hold of the instrument and led me through the crowd of employees, contractors, and the other select guests who'd come to the party.

On our leisurely walk, he snuck a few cookies from the kitchen. "You know..." he said, coy but nonchalant.

I glanced over at him, at which point we both stopped and he flashed a controlled grin. I raised my eyebrows in question.

"I think it's time you open the present I got you." He still held my violin, but he wrapped his arms around my lower back, pulling me against his broad chest, looking at me like a man in love. The way he'd looked at me so many times over the years, though so much more pronounced. "It might contain a few of the things that piqued your interest."

And he already knew by my smile and the way I bit my lower lip that I had my suspicions about what it contained. I flicked my wrist as though swinging the crop.

"You just have to open it and find out," he said, leaning his face down as I raised onto my toes for one of those kisses I loved. Him saying, "I love the buttercream frosting on your lips."

He would soon discover that a present I had waiting for him beneath the tree contained a pint of the sweet frosting for him to lick off any part of me he wanted to. And I would make sure there were supplies of the delicious icing year-round.